WALT DISNEY PRODUCTIONS
presents

Snow White
and the Messy Dwarfs

Random House  New York

Snow White and her prince lived happily in a big castle.

There were beautiful gardens and woods all around the castle.

Snow White liked to sing with the birds and play with the animals.

Most of all, Snow White liked to be
with her prince.
They loved each other very much.
Some days they had picnics
in the garden.

Some days they rode through the woods.
And some evenings they danced
until late at night.

One day the prince said, "Snow White,
I must go away for a few days."

Snow White looked sad.

"Why don't you visit
the seven dwarfs while
I am away? I will take
you to their house,"
said the prince.

"What a good idea!"
Snow White said.

Early the next day, Snow White
and the prince were ready to leave.
    "What is in your basket?"
the prince asked Snow White.
    "It is a special surprise
I've made for the dwarfs,"
said Snow White.

Snow White and the prince rode
through the forest all day.

At last they came to the home
of the seven dwarfs.

"Look! There are your friends!"
said the prince.

The seven dwarfs were so happy to see
Snow White!

Each dwarf greeted her in his own way.

Dopey jumped
for joy.

Sneezy sneezed
a loud sneeze.

Doc made
a little speech.
Grumpy just
looked grumpy.

Happy sang
a happy song.
Sleepy tried
to look awake.

And Bashful blushed.

"We'll take good care of Snow White
until you return," Doc said to the prince.
"Good-bye—we'll see you in two days!"

"What do you have
in your basket?"
Doc asked Snow White.
"It's a surprise,"
said Snow White.

"But you can't have
it until after supper,"
Snow White added.

"I think it is time
for supper now," said Doc.

It was night by the time supper was ready.
The dwarfs slurped down their hot stew.
"Dopey, use your spoon!" said Snow White.

Soon supper was finished.

"Now show us
the surprise!"
said Happy.

Snow White opened the basket.
Inside was a big chocolate cake.
"I made it just for you!" said Snow White.
"It's our favorite!" said the dwarfs.
They each had a big piece of cake.

Then the dwarfs played merry tunes
on their musical instruments.
Snow White sang and danced.
"What fun this is!" Snow White said.

Many hours passed.
Sleepy yawned.
"It has been fun,
but I am sleepy now,"
Sleepy said.

"Go to bed," said Snow White.
"It is late and you must work
tomorrow. I will wash the dishes."
    The seven dwarfs said good night.
Then they marched up to bed.

Snow White was sleepy too.
But the dishes were waiting
to be washed.
Snow White opened the door
to the kitchen.

Dirty dishes were
everywhere!
"What a mess!"
said Snow White.

Snow White washed
all the dishes, cups,
pots, and pans.

Then she scrubbed
the floor.

Finally
the kitchen
was clean.
It was late
at night.
Snow White
was very tired.

In the morning the dwarfs woke up and got dressed.

"Ssh!" whispered Doc. "Do not wake Snow White. Let her get a good rest."

The dwarfs ate a big breakfast.
Then they marched off to work.

"Time to get up, Snow White,"
sang a bluebird on the window sill.
"Good morning, little bird,"
said Snow White. "What a lovely day!
I think I will have a picnic lunch
in the woods today."

"But first I will clean the rest
of the house," Snow White said. "That
will be a nice surprise for the dwarfs."

Snow White
went downstairs
to the kitchen.

There was a surprise for Snow White
in the kitchen.

But it was not a nice surprise.

Dirty dishes covered the table.

A puddle of milk was on the floor.

"Those messy dwarfs!" said Snow White.

"Now I must clean the kitchen again!"

Snow White's animal friends helped.
Soon the dirty dishes were clean.

Then Snow White
swept the floor.
"Now to clean
everything else,"
said Snow White.

Snow White's friends
helped her some more.

A squirrel dusted
the cobwebs.

A little deer helped Snow White
to wash the dwarfs' clothes.

Finally all the cleaning was done.
Snow White thanked her animal friends.
"I could not have done it without you,"
Snow White said to them.

The dwarfs had worked hard all day.
They set off for home.

"I bet Snow White has dinner waiting
for us!" said Doc.

"I hope it's not spinach!" said Grumpy.

"Snow White, we're home!" called the seven dwarfs.

"I do not smell dinner cooking," said Doc. "And where is Snow White?"

"Maybe she is sleeping
upstairs," said Grumpy.

The dwarfs ran upstairs
to Snow White's bedroom.

Snow White was sitting on her bed.
"Are you sick?" asked the dwarfs.
"No," said Snow White. "I'm tired."

"Tired from cooking
a wonderful dinner?"
asked Doc.

"No," said Snow White. "I am tired from cleaning your messy house!"

"We're sorry," the dwarfs said. "We didn't mean to make you tired or unhappy. What can we do?"

"If you help me, dinner will be ready in no time," said Snow White.

Sleepy got the milk.

Bashful peeled the potatoes.

Happy carried the soup.

Dopey and Sneezy set the table.

Doc gave orders.

And Grumpy watched.

Soon dinner was ready.

The next morning, Snow White woke up
early.

"I will surprise the dwarfs today.
I'll make them a nice breakfast,"
Snow White said. "But I'll be very quiet
so they don't wake up."

Snow White tiptoed past the dwarfs' room.
But the dwarfs were already up!
They had made their beds.
Their slippers were beneath their stools.
Snow White was very surprised.

Another surprise was in the kitchen.
"Good morning! We have made breakfast.
Now it is our turn to do the housework,"
the dwarfs said to Snow White.

The prince arrived after breakfast.
Snow White said good-bye to the dwarfs.
"Come again soon!" called the dwarfs.
Snow White and the prince rode away.
"Now who will clean up the dishes
from breakfast?" asked Grumpy.
"All of us!" said Doc. "We've learned
that everything is easier if we all help!"